E
T2865w

To Marco and Matilde

First published in the United States by
Dial Books for Young Readers
A Division of E. P. Dutton
A Division of New American Library
2 Park Avenue
New York, New York 10016
Published in Great Britain by Andersen Press
Copyright © 1986 by Fulvio Testa
All rights reserved
Printed in Italy
Design by Atha Tehon
First Edition
U S

10 9 8 7 6 5 4 3 2 1
Library of Congress Cataloging in Publication Data
Testa, Fulvio. Wolf's favor.
Summary: By doing a simple favor for Porcupine, Wolf sets off an
unnatural chain of good deeds from stronger animals to weaker ones.
[1. Animals—Fiction. 2. Kindness—Fiction.] I. Title.
PZ7.T2875Wo   1986   [E]   85–15934
ISBN 0–8037–0244–2

The art for each picture consists of an ink and dye painting,
which is camera-separated and reproduced in full color.

WOLF'S FAVOR

FULVIO TESTA

Dial Books for Young Readers ◇ New York

One day Porcupine found a big nut in the forest. Her mouth watered as she thought of how good it would taste. But no matter how hard she tried, Porcupine could not get the nut open. At last she went to see Wolf.

"Good morning, Wolf. How well you are looking this morning," said Porcupine.

Wolf narrowed his eyes and said nothing.

"I wonder if you would do me a favor and open this nut," Porcupine went on. "Your teeth are so strong and sharp, it would only take you a moment."

"You're lucky I have already had my breakfast, Porcupine. Don't you know I could eat you up in one bite?" said Wolf.

At this Porcupine backed away in alarm.

"Wait," said Wolf. "Because I admire your courage, today I will help you." Then he took the nut in his huge mouth and cracked it open with his powerful teeth.

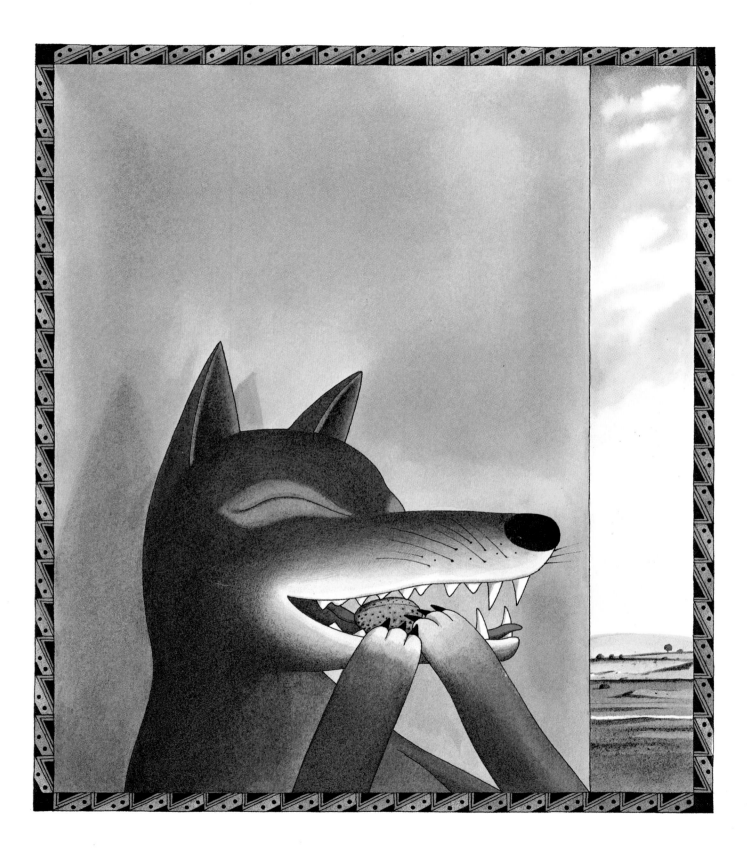

"Thank you," said Porcupine.

"Not at all," answered Wolf, plucking one of her quills. "I don't think I've ever done anyone a favor before. It's been very interesting."

Not wanting to bother Wolf further, Porcupine said good-bye and went off to eat her nut.

It was not long before Squirrel joined her. "How did you get that nut open?" he asked, staring longingly at it.

"Wolf did me a favor and opened it," said Porcupine.

"Wolf did you a favor, all right. He did you a favor not to eat you!" said Squirrel.

But Porcupine only shrugged. Her adventure was over and now she wanted to eat. "There's enough here for two, Squirrel. Have a piece if you'd like."

Quickly, before Porcupine could change her mind, Squirrel took a piece of the nut and went back to his favorite tree. As he ate it, a few crumbs fell.

Then Squirrel heard a loud *caw*, *caw* and Crow landed near him. Squirrel, of course, knew just why he was there.

"If you want the crumbs, Crow, you can have them," said Squirrel. "Wolf did a favor for Porcupine and Porcupine did a favor for me. Why shouldn't I be generous too?"

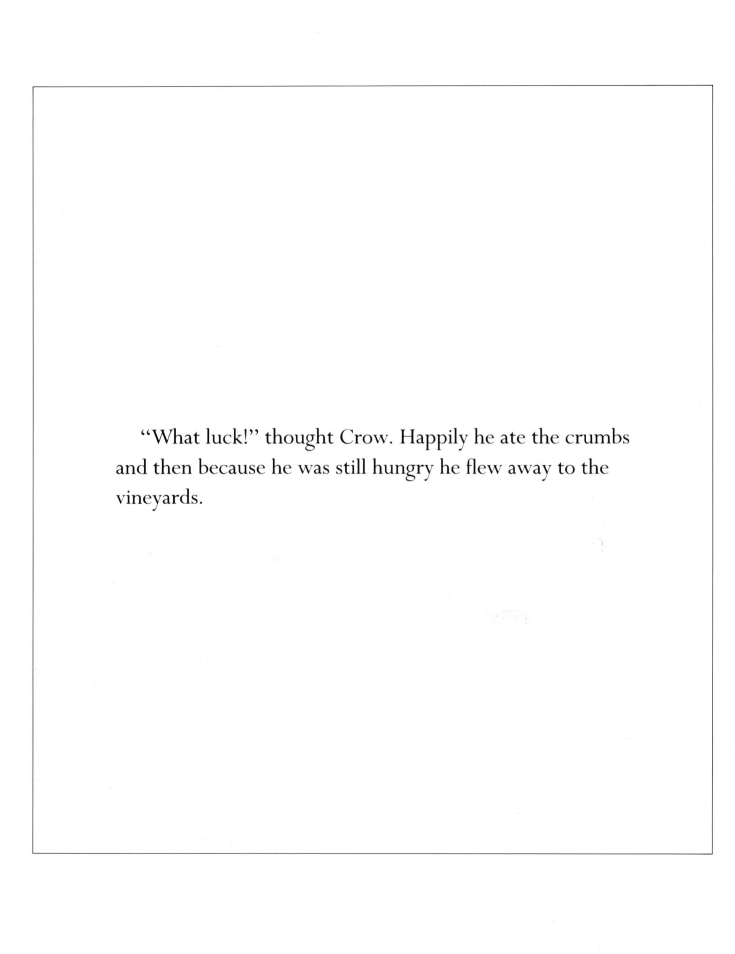

"What luck!" thought Crow. Happily he ate the crumbs and then because he was still hungry he flew away to the vineyards.

When he got there, he saw Fox.

"Fox, I know you cannot reach those grapes, so if you'd like I will pick some for you," said Crow.

"Why would you do that?" asked Fox suspiciously.

"Let's just say that everyone has been doing favors for everyone else and it won't hurt to give you some grapes. Especially now that I don't want any myself," said Crow.

Peck, peck, peck. Suddenly out came Chicken. But when she saw Fox, she started to run away.

"There's no need to go, Chicken," said Fox, putting the last grape in her mouth. "Because Crow did a favor for me, I've decided to do a favor for you. I won't eat you— at least not today."

Chicken was relieved but so confused that she forgot where she was going and ran around in circles.

Then Snake, who had been watching from a tree, asked Chicken why Fox had not eaten her.

"I really don't understand," she answered. "But it has something to do with a favor done to Crow by Fox or Fox by Crow, I can't remember." And Chicken wandered off, pecking at the ground.

Snake wondered what it would be like to do someone a favor. But he knew very well that the others disliked him and would never ask for his help.

Just then he saw Lamb. "Ah-ha," thought Snake and he slithered down the tree trunk.

"Good day, Lamb," he said. "I would like to do you a favor. Tell me what you need."

"I don't need anything, really. When I have just a little grass, I am content," answered Lamb.

"I see," said Snake. "Then you must go to a field I know where the grass grows green and tender. It's just on the other side of those trees."

"Thank you," said Lamb, touched by Snake's kindness.

Snake was pleased to have done Lamb a favor and,
of course, Lamb was even more pleased when she saw the
beautiful field and began to eat the sweet green grass.

Meanwhile, some distance away, Wolf was thinking that the favor he'd done for Porcupine had made him feel so good that he wanted to do one more favor. So instead of hunting for his next meal, Wolf lay down in the hot sunshine to take a little nap.